About this book

Many children have difficulty puzzling out letters because they
are abstract symbols. Letterland's worldwide success is all about its
enduring characters who give these symbols life and stop them from being
abstract. In this book we meet the Hairy Hat Man. His story is carefully
designed to emphasise the sounds that the letter 'H' makes in words.
This definitive, original story book is an instant collector's classic,
making learning fun for a new generation of readers.

A TEMPLAR BOOK

This edition published in the UK in 2008 by Templar Publishing
an imprint of The Templar Company plc,
The Granary, North Street, Dorking, Surrey, RH4 1DN, UK
www.templarco.co.uk

First published by Hamlyn Publishing, 1985
Devised and produced by The Templar Company plc

1 3 5 7 9 8 6 4 2

ISBN 978-1-84011-780-6

Printed in China

Classic LETTERLAND
Storybooks

The Hairy Hat Man's House

Written by Lyn Wendon

Illustrated by
Jane Launchbury

templar publishing

BRACKNELL FOREST
BOROUGH COUNCIL

Harry was a little boy who loved hats. Little hats, big hats, tall hats and short hats. Anything he could put on his head made him happy. As he grew older, collecting hats became his hobby. Soon he had nearly a hundred hats.

When Harry became a man, he still loved hats. So one day he started a hat shop in the little house where he lived, half way up a hill.

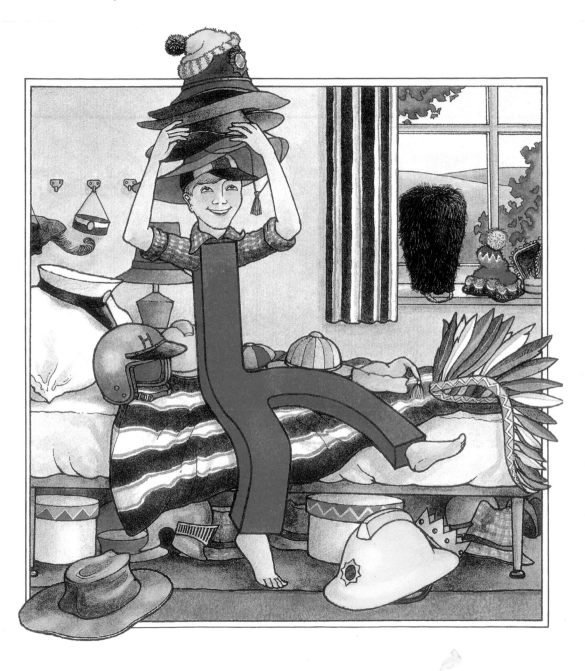

Lots of people came to buy hats from his hat shop. They could buy any hat they wanted, except one. That was because one of Harry's hats was not for sale.

It was his favourite hat – a green, rather hairy hat. He had made it himself and he wore it all the time.

Soon people stopped calling him Harry. They always called him the 'Hairy Hat Man' instead.

The Hairy Hat man lived happily
in his little house, until one
evening there was a great
storm in Letterland.
The wind blew hard and the rain
poured down. The storm was still
raging when he went to bed.
When he woke up the next morning
the poor Hat Man had a terrible shock.

"Heavens!" he cried. "The wind has
blown a hole in my roof.
Now all my hats are soaked!"

He carried the dripping hats outside
and hung them on the line to dry.
He felt very unhappy.

"**H**enry," he said to his horse, "where will I get the money to buy a new roof?"

"You'll just have to sell lots more hats," said Henry.

"But how?" asked the Hairy Hat Man. "It is a long walk up the hill to my hat shop. I can't make the hill any shorter, can I?"

"You could take the hats down the hill and sell them in the market!" said Henry.

"But how will I ever carry them all?" asked the Hairy Hat Man.
"By horse?" suggested Henry, smiling.
"What a good idea!" cried Harry.

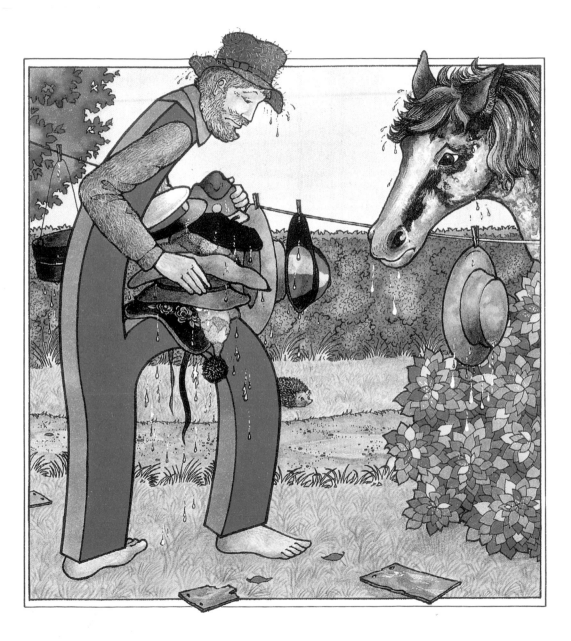

As soon as his hats were dry,
the Hairy Hat Man harnessed
Henry to a cart and loaded it
high with hats. Together they set off
down the hill.

In the market place it was very busy.
The Hairy Hat Man stopped the
cart to give Henry some hay.

Soon lots of people had gathered
round to buy hats. It was hot work,
but the Hat Man and Henry hoped to
sell enough hats to pay for a new roof
before it rained again.

Every day they worked in the market place. They sold so many hats that soon the people had all the hats they needed... but the Hat Man STILL did not have enough money for a new roof.

"It's hopeless," he said to his horse. "I don't know what to do now, Henry."

Henry's ears twitched as he tried to think.
"I can't think in this hot sun," he said. "Please make me a sun hat!"

"What a good idea!" said Harry.
So straight away he made a large sun hat for Henry, with two holes in just the right places for his ears.

Soon all the other horses in Letterland heard about Henry's hat. They wanted to buy sun hats, too.

The next day, Bouncy Ben came along and asked, "Can you make me a special baseball cap?"

"I'd be happy to," said Hairy Hat Man. So he made a special baseball cap for Bouncy Ben, with two holes in just the right places for his ears.

When Bouncy Ben's brothers saw his baseball cap, they all wanted one just like it. So the Hat Man made special caps for them too.

The next day, Clever Cat came along. She liked Henry's hat very much. "Can you make me a special cat hat?" she asked.

"Of course," said the Hat Man. So he made a special cat hat for her, with two holes in just the right places for her ears.

When Clever Cat's cousins saw her special hat they all wanted to buy one too. So Harry made lots more.

Soon the Hairy Hat Man had made a special hat for almost every animal in Letterland. But he STILL did not have enough money for the new roof.

"**H**enry," he said to his horse one day. "There is still only enough money for half a roof. We'll never have enough before it rains again. NOW what shall we do?"

Henry's ears twitched in their hat holes as he thought. Then he had an idea.

"If you can make sun hats for heads," he said, "why can't you make a rain hat for your house?"

"Of course!" cried the Hairy Hat Man, hopping up and down with excitement. "I could make a huge rain hat! If I make it myself it won't cost very much at all!"

That very same day he started to make a special hat for his house. It was huge, and it had two holes in just the right places for his chimneys.

When it was finished, his Letterland friends helped to put the new hat on his house.

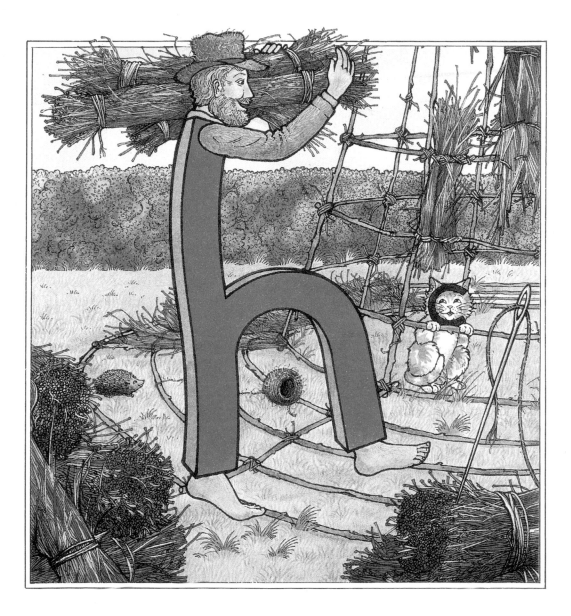

At last the Hairy Hat Man was happy again. Now it didn't matter if it rained... his house had a new roof!

"Everyone likes my new roof, don't they, Henry!" he said to his horse.

Henry smiled. "That's because it looks like your favourite hat," said Henry.

The Hairy Hat Man looked at his new roof again. "It does rather, doesn't it," he said, smiling happily.

THE END